Unlock Your Heart
Goal Setting From The Inside Out

By

Jane Ellen Davis

Copyright © 2001 by Jane Ellen Davis
All rights reserved.
No part of this book may be reproduced, restored in a retrieval system, or transmitted by means, electronic, mechanical, photocopying, recording, or otherwise, without written consent from the author.

ISBN: 0-75962-908-0

This book is printed on acid free paper.

Gratitude and Acknowledgment

I would like to express my gratitude to my father, Claud Sympson, for his complete support in all my endeavors. To my mother, Jimmie, who loved and honored my creativity, I am deeply indebted. I humbly acknowledge my two sons, Andy and Zack, who are embracing their creative talents and living lives rich in possibility. To friends and clients who practiced the principles presented in this guidebook and permitted me to use their life experiences as examples for others to follow, I give my thanks.

Specifically, I extend deep gratitude to my intuitive editor and friend, Parthenia Hicks. Her understanding and encouragement provided me with courage and fortitude.

To Darlene Hollingsworth, my dear friend and traveling storyteller, I give thanks for countless hours on the computer, doing the formatting and "stuff" I hate to do! And—for never losing faith in the principles I am presenting here.

I am very grateful to Linda Phillips, another visionary, who designed the cover art and shared her computer graphic skills unselfishly.

Supreme thanks go to Sharon Draper, Kathryn Retzler and Dee Hoffman, soul sisters from way back, who never lost sight of the dream. And—to seekers of self-discovery, whoever you are, I say, continue!

Introduction

If you were drawn to pick up this book you are probably someone who actively "does" your life. Yet you desire more—more fulfillment, less stress and effort. I can relate! Much of my life has been spent going through the motions and not being fully aware of why I have been doing what I was doing or what result I really desired based on all that "doing." I knew there had to be more to life than just busy activities without much purpose. I knew that gaining a deeper understanding of myself and what I really wanted from life was the key.

The more I work with people from all walks of life, the more I realize we each have a dream, a longing, quietly simmering inside, that yearns to burst out and express itself. We all have unique qualities and God-given talents. Life is all about learning to appreciate ourselves and discovering ways to tap into our natural, internal reservoir of skills, talents, ideas, feelings and intuition. Somehow, the daily requirements of living fog up our self-image and hinder our progress. In order to earn a living, provide for all those who need us, and stay afloat, we neglect the introspection necessary to nurture self-growth.

So, for the past twenty years I have spent a great deal of my time, energy and resources studying and applying the principles taken from an incredible personal journey of seminars, classrooms, workshops, psychotherapy, intense introspection and basic soul searching. Along the path I have picked up some ideas, some principles to live by and some rare experiences to cherish—nothing grandiose or extraordinary, just simple practices that work for me. I have learned to create what I want, to communicate my intentions, to balance my emotional prosperity with my physical input, and to trust my instincts. As a result of this, I believe I can be a catalyst for others to discover their natural gifts and talents and to create personal satisfaction and joy in their lives. This has become my life's work.

I have brought my life's lessons together in the form of a workbook for study and reflection. My goal is for this workbook to provide motivation, re-enlightenment and reinforcement of personal values.

My challenge has been to create a workbook that gives you permission to study yourself and approach life with a smile while imparting practical ideas and applications to enable you to achieve the results you want.

I do not profess to have all the answers. What I do have is a tremendous amount of love and warmth to share in the form of ideas and techniques designed to allow you to feel better about yourself and the challenges and opportunities in your life.

Spend some time absorbing what is here. Put it to the test in your own experience. A wonderful poet and counselor, Rusty Berkus, sums up my philosophy beautifully by saying, "Life is a party to which you have been invited. Are you going to sit on the sidelines, or join in the dance?"

Purpose of This Book

The purpose of this workbook is to provide a methodology for you to follow and practice that will allow you to discover who you are *naturally* and what you desire, by operating from the space of who you really are.

You probably know instinctively when you are being natural. There is no contrived behavior. You are not putting on a front or acting in a manner that is not really authentic. You are honest with yourself and others. You are openly expressing your joys as well as your concerns or fears. You are self-confident and have clarity of purpose— in other words, you know what you want and you can create it. You do not experience fatigue. Your actions become easier and you generate a natural enthusiasm because you are *being* your unique, creative self. Your goals unfold effortlessly; there is no limit to the degree of energy you devote to an activity.

This workbook is designed to help you re-evaluate the way you think of yourself and your abilities—to help you clarify who you are.

The intention of this transformational guidebook is to:

1) Discover your natural gifts and talents by unlocking your heart.
2) Experience this shift in how you see yourself.
3) Begin creating the life you always wanted.

Discovering and uncovering your natural self can lead to a new way of being that automatically generates powerful possibilities.

How To Use This Book

Begin by reading the introduction and start with Session One. The sessions are in sequence and a pattern will unfold as you proceed through each session. Each session takes you into the next progression in your transformational process, like a dance.

Use a notebook or yellow pad as you read each session. Keep a dictionary handy and look up any word you are unsure about.

Do the exercises that are included in each session. It will be best to do a session each week until you have completed all seven sessions. If you find a session particularly challenging or compelling, stay with it until you feel a sense of clarity and understanding. These sessions can be quite intense because each one is designed to make you think about yourself and your life, and to discover insights that will empower you. Many times these insights will require you to take certain actions, which will be addressed in the session. There will be exercises and steps for you to follow to give you guidance and peace of mind.

One excellent method for using this book is to form a group of six or eight people and study the sessions together on a weekly basis. Group study can be very empowering and supportive. Depending on the type of group you assemble, the length of time it will take to complete the sessions will vary. One person can act as facilitator each time you meet. The benefit of creating a study group is that the mutual energy the group provides allows goals and possibilities to be fully recognized.

Unlock Your Heart: Goal Setting from the Inside Out

Session One

<u>Unlocking Your Values</u>

Who are you when you are at your best? If you were to describe the characteristics and attributes you display when you know you are *being the best you can be*, what descriptive words would you use? Begin by getting a picture in your mind of you performing a task you love, presenting an idea, playing your favorite game or sport, expressing love, or any other activity where you shine. See yourself there. Notice the way you are behaving in that moment. Begin to describe your actions. Are you graceful? Are you peaceful? Are you energized? Is your body fully present and balanced? Describe everything you notice about yourself. Write down what you notice. Within that description are your core values. You are those values when you are manifesting your natural gifts and talents.

Jane Ellen Davis

Who I Am at My Best

_____

_____

_____

In this first session we will begin to explore who you really are in terms of what you value. We begin here because goals determined from your personal set of values take on a whole new energy compared to your old, limited goals. You are approaching goals from a new focus. Instead of forming goals that come from the need to do something to cause the goal to happen, your goals will transpire based upon who you are *being.* The definition of a goal used throughout this workbook is: purposeful intentions and possibilities specifically stated on paper, affirmed visually, actively pursed, with no attachment to the outcome. As we proceed through the sessions you will see how this definition applies. Once you have identified your core values, your goals become very clear. You are then motivated to apply strong intention to achieving what you want. Intention is an intangible quality. It is a knowingness that comes from understanding quite clearly what it is you

Unlock Your Heart: Goal Setting from the Inside Out

want. From that clarity, you are able to project your thoughts so that they become productive energy. This clear thought combines with your action and the outcome reaches far beyond your original desire.

Basically what you are doing is projecting a thought toward a desired result. The closer the connection between your intention and your core values, the greater the outcome. When you have this clarity, your powerful intention combines with your inner resources and you discover your own connection to universal energy.

The deepest qualities you believe in are your core values—what really matters to you when everything else is out of the way. Once you define what you value and begin manifesting those values, your daily experience takes on a whole new meaning. The more in touch you are with your values, the smoother and easier your creative processes will be.

Discovering these core values begins by reflecting on achievements. Think of an accomplishment you are most proud of and how energized that accomplishment made you feel. Now, think of a time when you achieved a goal you didn't really care about and how all you felt was relief or exhaustion. Those accomplishments that were exciting and empowering for you were honoring your core values. Goals that transpire out of your core values are goals that make your heart sing. These heart-oriented desires for fulfillment create in you powerful energy to provide the action within the goal. When you unlock your values—what you believe in about yourself—you will learn that honoring them is the first step to manifesting your goals.

Believing in yourself enough to take the risk of following your core values is a powerful key to creating goals that are centered internally.

This is transformational because as a result of choosing to follow your personal values, you become what it is you want. This is a natural transformation that automatically unfolds based upon who you are *being*. So the old way of goal setting and then doing something to accomplish that goal is shifted. The shift begins with the discovery of what is in your heart—what you value, what you really want, what your higher self is gifted to *be* in life. Once this discovery is clear, goals automatically transpire out of your clarity and powerful intention. They take on an effortless, magical manifestation.

Unlock Your Heart: Goal Setting from the Inside Out

Take a few minutes now and list at least five accomplishments. Once you have listed them read through the list several times. Within each accomplishment there will be a certain quality that becomes obvious to you. Once you discover what that quality is you can unlock the core value within that quality.

For example: This past year one of my greatest accomplishments was improving the communication between my youngest son and myself. Our communication usually consisted of him being defensive and me being the Questioning Mom. I made a conscious choice to no longer quiz him about his actions and choices. I chose to listen to him without judgment. I decided to honor his choices and let go of my pre-assessments of his behavior. After making those decisions I began listening differently, honoring his words, listening for his joy, excitement, self-worth, purposeful activity and expressions of his creativity. As a result of my non-judgmental listening, I began to feel love flowing through me. It took some time but a huge shift in our communication happened. We now communicate honestly, joyfully appreciating each other. I now get to share in his passion for his life; his personal picture of what life is for him, without my idea of what it should be.

As I read through this accomplishment, I noticed that once I let go of my judgments of my son, what showed up was my own core value of Unconditional Love. So I learned that an extremely important value for me is love without judgment—just pure love for love's sake.

I also discovered that letting go, or being willing to give up certain ideas or ways of being, created an immediate, positive shift. In other words, being willing to drop an old way of behaving that limited progress and caused upsets, allowed for a new, fresh, creative ability to surface.

List of Accomplishments

1) _____
2) _____
3) _____
4) _____
5) _____

Unlock Your Heart: Goal Setting from the Inside Out

Here's another example from Pat, a client of mine who is a very successful real estate broker. Her list of accomplishments looked like this!

1) White water rafting trip
2) Doubling her real estate income
3) Putting a new deck on her home
4) Going on vacation over Christmas instead of working
5) Being single

As you can see, her accomplishments are varied and certainly demonstrate what she values about herself and her life. Your accomplishments will reflect your own unique life, as Pat's and mine do.

As you look over your list of accomplishments, notice the personal values that exist within each accomplishment. Those values are who you are. They are the core of your *being*. They are the attributes of your natural gifts and talents. See if you can create a list of five of your personal values. Some examples might be: Love, Integrity, Freedom, Honesty, Harmony, and Health. Using Pat as an example again: After examining her accomplishments, she realized she valued Adventure (which involved stretching herself, risk taking), Service to others (which demonstrated Love, Honoring Others and Integrity), Beauty (the richness of the human spirit), Family and Freedom (no limits-independence). Review her list of accomplishments and see if you can understand why she chose these values. Can you begin to get a sense of her power and the kind of contributions she makes based upon knowing what she values?

List of Your Core Values

1) _____
2) _____
3) _____
4) _____
5) _____

How often do you really stop and consider what you value about your life? Most of us sort of know on some deeper level that we value our freedom and our privacy as

Unlock Your Heart: Goal Setting from the Inside Out

individuals, but we certainly do not dwell on the thought consciously.

If you were to consider for a few moments what is truly important to you, what would show up? For instance, what's important to you in a relationship—say with a family member or a child, or perhaps a loved one outside of the family? Your values are an integral part of that importance. Those values need to be present and acknowledged in who you are on a daily basis. Suppose you are a business executive and one of your deepest values is personal integrity—that essence of whatever integrity means to you must be a part of who you are *being* in all your activities, business-related or not. In order for you to experience the ability to perform with excellence, and the benefits that performance produces, you must be tuned in to your personal integrity and manifesting those values.

The joy, enthusiasm and richness of life evolve out of *being* what it is you value. Taking the time to evaluate all those attributes that are deeply entrenched in the fiber of your being will pay off immensely. Once you can truly claim those amazing values, your entire way of operating in life shifts. You become those values. People will respect you when you are honoring your values. They will begin to emulate that behavior and in a sense, clean up their own act.

The first time you choose to consciously exemplify your values and incorporate them in your daily actions will be astounding. Not only will your personal enthusiasm escalate, the reaction from others will delight you. They will wake up and pay attention to you. They will be more present, less critical, more expressive, and more enthusiastic of your ideas. The creative energy emerging from your personal commitment to your values will enroll others automatically in a much bigger, richer, more beneficial way of *being* that contributes to everyone involved.

It is easy to enroll someone else in enthusiasm when it is naturally radiating from you. I am certain you have experienced what I am talking about at one time or another. Perhaps as a child on the playground at recess you were excited about a game of tag. So you started laughing and chasing someone and the game began. Your energy and delight in the chase attracted someone else—and then others saw what fun you were having and joined in. We've all been there, caught up in an energy-charged event wanting to connect to that adrenaline high that comes from active play, wanting that carefree, vibrant joy that happens in a moment of pure creativity!

Let's reflect for a few moments on your playtime at five or six years old. Give yourself about a half hour to do this exercise. Find a place where you can get quiet and not be disturbed. Relax and take several deep breaths. Continue concentrating on your breathing and feel your body quiet down. Let your mind take you to a playtime when you were five or six. Be sure to recall a pleasant playtime. Once you get a vivid picture of where you were and whom you were with, notice exactly what you were doing. See how carefree and spontaneous you were as you played. Listen to the sounds and see the sights around you. Recapture the joy and exuberance of uninhibited play. Take a few moments and watch yourself playing. Were you a tree climber, a cowboy or girl, did you love to paint or color? Whatever you did in your playtime is who you are naturally. All that joy and freedom is still available to you when you respond to your natural creativity. You can re-create it anytime you choose to do so.

Jane Ellen Davis

Play Exercise: Write a brief paragraph of what you saw as you reflected on your playful times in childhood. Pay special attention to the attributes and creative energy you had naturally. Several attributes will probably show up. No doubt one of them will be an expression of personal freedom. What a joy it was to be in a non-judgmental place, just *being you.*

_____

_____

_____

Read through what you have written. Notice the descriptive words you used. Underline any attributes or personal values you mentioned in your description. Then look into your present situation and see if any of those values and marvelous creative traits is still part of your life.

Make a note of where they are still a part of your life and where they are missing. Look at your personal relationships, your career, your spirituality, and your time alone. For many of us, the obvious void shows up. Our personal freedom has been surrendered to a way of life that does not allow for our creative energy to shine.

Unlock Your Heart: Goal Setting from the Inside Out

Take a moment now to decide how you can begin manifesting your personal values and delightful playfulness into your daily experience. Write about it as if you are already behaving this way and it is making a difference.

When you are consciously aware of your core values, this creative energy is available and actively functioning within you. All you need to do is tap into it and trust yourself.

What you will notice is a sense of flowing through an activity, almost as if you are detached from the doingness of it. The activity seems effortless. *There is no concern or fear of failure present.* There is no mental chatter pulling your attention toward any potential hazards and pitfalls. There are no self-doubts or old tapes playing in your head. You are pure creative energy flowing in perfect synergy. You are being fully present, totally trusting what you know naturally.

Michael Jordan, when he played basketball, was probably the greatest example of this kind of flawless *beingness.* He was *being* his natural gift when he created those awesome moves on the court. Certainly he is an amazing athlete, but we all have natural gifts. These gifts are available and are an intrinsic part of our makeup. Michael knows and believes in his abilities and totally trusts his divine heritage—and the rest of us can, too.

That effortless performance is available at all times. Most of us only experience it in fleeting moments and even then we do not trust it. Our mind overwhelms us with all the reasons it won't ever be possible again. The key is to learn how to notice the mind chatter, acknowledge it for speaking to you and protecting you, and assure it that you are fully in charge and choose to continue to trust your natural ability. In other words, you control the mind's contribution; it does not control you.

This takes practice and constant vigilance. The mind is always present and ready to take over, and the mind can make brilliant contributions when you are guiding it from your natural intuitive awareness. You are not letting it run the "I'm not good enough" video. Once you begin to experience this wonderful flow of natural creative ability, like that of Michael Jordan, you can also begin to enjoy it and absorb it into your daily life. It becomes intrinsically a part of you. The energy is always there waiting for you to tap into and acknowledge it.

Unlock Your Heart: Goal Setting from the Inside Out

Let me present an exercise for taking charge of the mental chatter that can inhibit you from using your natural gifts.

1) When the mind starts with its negative chatter, immediately take charge by acknowledging it. Say, "Thank you for talking with me about your concerns." Listen carefully to what it says. Emotions will show up if you listen quietly and deeply enough. The secret of the underlying pain, fear, anger and sadness is what ultimately stops you from creating your brilliant future. Identify the emotion that surfaces. Let yourself feel it deeply. Continue to stay with that emotion and let it run its course. Then say, "Thank you for sharing and caring about me. I understand your concern for my welfare. You do not need to protect me. I am in charge and I am choosing to trust my natural talent and perform from that trust." There may be more than one emotion that surfaces, so you may have to repeat the process for each one. Once you have processed all the emotions you are ready for the next step.

2) Ask the mind to join you and assist you in your performance. What you are doing is engaging the mind to work with you instead of against you. Think about the best way the mind can contribute to what you want to accomplish. Tell the mind how it can help you. For instance, you might say, "I am about to make a presentation to a group and I need to be well organized and focused. I need to be enthusiastic and clear in what I say."
3) Once you have completed your activity honor the mind by thanking it for being there for you. Say it. Really get connected and feel the complete communication you took charge of.
4) Acknowledge yourself for being in charge and educating your mind to work with you.

The more you practice this format, the easier it becomes and the more naturally it will take shape for you. It will become something you automatically do when you notice you are in your head and not fully present. It can be one of your most valuable tools in self-communication.

Unlock Your Heart: Goal Setting from the Inside Out

Once you have identified who you are at your best, look again at your list of core values. Try to select three of the most important values. Base your selection on those values that excite, energize and create passion for you. The three values that come forth for me are Creativity, Freedom of Expression, and Abundance of Love. Pat's three most core values were: Adventure, Beauty and Love.

Your core values may be quite different. The values you choose make up the essence of who you are. Write down your three most important values. Which values excite, energize and create passion in you?

List Your Three Most Important Core Values

1) _____
2) _____
3) _____

Notice where they show up or occur in your present life. Write down the areas in your life where you can see that those core values are an integral part of your experience.

Jane Ellen Davis

Where Are Your Core Values in Your Present Life?

1) _____
2) _____
3) _____

Notice also where your core values are not being expressed. Many of you will have a rude awakening here. For some, those most important core values will be missing more often than they will be present.

Pat discovered where her values were not being expressed.

1) Daily life gets ho-hum.
2) An exciting, passionate relationship with a man.
3) Being outdoors enjoying the beauty of nature.
4) The benefits of meditation.

Areas Where Core Values Are Not Being Expressed

1) _____
2) _____

Unlock Your Heart: Goal Setting from the Inside Out

It is up to you to choose to integrate your values into your current life. In order to do that, you need to create a purpose, a reason for *being* those values. Your purpose is the why of what you do. It is intrinsically woven into your deepest aspects. You live it rather than have it. It gives your life meaning and is the basis for who you are with others and how you respond in your daily interaction. *Your purpose is connected to your core values and is the basis for all your goals.*

My Life Purpose is motivated by my passion to be a guide or catalyst for others to discover their natural creativity—thus manifesting an abundance of love in their lives by believing in the possibility of the freedom to *be* that creativity. Knowing this is my personal purpose allows me to structure my actions accordingly. I can connect this same purpose to all areas of my life. Therefore, I must express love, freedom and natural creative energy in who I am *being*. If I choose to exhibit those values in my actions moment to moment, I encourage and inspire others to be their personal passion. My life evolves more naturally when I am sure of my purpose. If I deliberately plan my actions based on my personal purpose, the experiences I have are filled with a sense of peace and clarity.

Our ability to stay focused with the intention to *be* in the moment, expressing our values, can be limited by our lack of experience in just *being* rather than feeling compelled to do something at all times. When we are *being*, all our values are evidenced in our activities, and the doing happens effortlessly. I am not implying that in order to just *be*, you curtail all activity and sit on a rock. As you discover how powerful you are when you are *being* and manifesting *as* your values, you will want to embrace those attributes and become closely aligned with them. The more you are aware of your purpose, what you truly believe about yourself and what you want to create, the greater your personal life experiences will be.

Take a few minutes now to reflect on your three values and see if you can discover and create a personal purpose. Compose an all-consuming purpose first, then your purposes within your life responsibilities, i.e., job/career, family, social relationships, spiritual life, etc. Remember to ask yourself "why do I want to manifest these values in all areas of my life?" That why is directly connected to your

Unlock Your Heart: Goal Setting from the Inside Out

purpose. If you find it too difficult to define your life purpose, focus on one area at a time such as job/career, etc. The clarity you derive from doing that will start you in the right direction. Then you will notice that your life purpose will carry over into all your other purposes because it clearly represents who you are.

Life Purpose

_____

_____

_____

_____

_____

_____

_____

Job/Career Purpose

_____

_____

_____

_____

_____

_____

_____

Jane Ellen Davis

Family Purpose

Social Purpose

Spiritual Purpose

Unlock Your Heart: Goal Setting from the Inside Out

Remember Pat? Her three values were Adventure, Beauty and Love. She created a passionate life purpose based on those three values. Her life purpose is to be living in the moment, expressing love, surrounded by beauty and free to trust the Universe. As she took a deeper look at her current life, she discovered she could incorporate that purpose into each realm of her life. Her career could take on a much more satisfying sense of purpose if she attempted each day to express love and trust herself to act accordingly. Her family life certainly could be more fulfilling and much more beauty would surround her if she manifested those love expressions with family members.

Once you can identify why you are who you are and why you chose to do what you do, you can spot immediately those aspects of your current life that are falling short of your purpose. For some, it may seem as if your whole life has been off-purpose.

The following exercise is designed to help you identify which areas of your life are already aligned with your purpose. Those areas that do not align with your purpose will be easy to discover.

Jane Ellen Davis

Wheel of Purpose

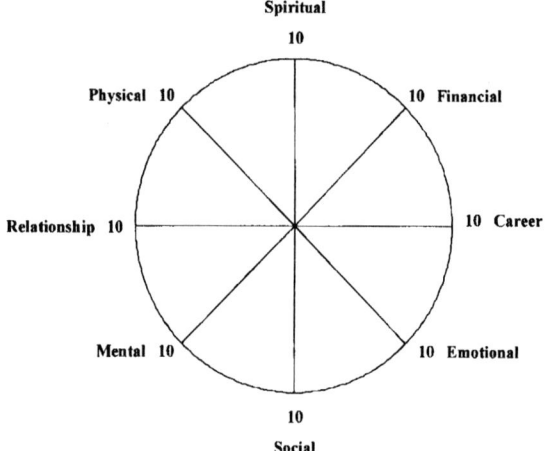

Place a dot on the line that best indicates where you are right now in each realm of your life. 0 being the lowest--10 being the highest. Then connect the dots. What do you see about your balance and purpose? What will it take to create a 10 in each area? Who will you need to *be*?

Unlock Your Heart: Goal Setting from the Inside Out

Notice Out of Balance Areas

___
___
___
___
___
___

Consider what it would take to create a "10" in each area.

Creating the "10" You Would Like to Become in Each Area

___
___
___
___
___
___
___

Making a conscious commitment to adopt your core values into your daily life will give you the motivation to begin taking charge of your choices.

You have, so far, listed your values, noted accomplishments in which those values played an integral role and identified your personal life purpose. If you find you still are uncertain about your deepest purpose, continue anyway. The more you absorb the processes in the upcoming sessions, the greater your clarity of purpose will be. DON'T BE DISCOURAGED!

Session Two is designed to assist and guide you in reclaiming your ability to choose. In order to be clear enough about your desire and your commitment to change, certain limiting beliefs must be released. Session Two will give you the opportunity to experience this release by presenting specific exercises to assist you.

Session Two

Stepping Out-Shedding the Old and Taking Charge

The insights that you may be starting to discover are getting you ready to begin making positive decisions that allow you to stay focused on your values and purpose. For some of you this decision-making process will not be easy because you have seldom experienced complete freedom to choose what you want. It is important to understand that you have a choice.

Choosing is, in a sense, taking charge. When you choose, you are being responsible. You are setting up your own circumstances, rather than just reacting to circumstances beyond your control. Choosing often causes the necessity to shift patterns that are no longer appropriate. Choosing usually means moving out of a comfort zone of predictable patterns and behavior into new uncharted territory where creative energy is always present. Having the trust and courage to step out into this empty space can bring forth fear and doubt. Once fear and doubt show up, hesitation and mental blocks step in and immobilize progress. All the old tapes begin to play and the creative flow is blocked. Session one mentioned this phenomenon and provided an exercise to assist in controlling it. In this session you will be given several exercises to assist you in handling this "old baggage." Keep in mind that this type of work can be very confronting and uncomfortable. Do the best you can to clear up as many of these past barriers as possible. Do the most obvious ones. **If you get too overwhelmed, move on to the next session.** Just be aware of these past issues and handle them as often as you can. This is not easy for most of us, but the outcome can be very rewarding and freeing.

Making wise choices requires trust. Trust plays a huge role in personal growth. You must establish trust in who you are before you can experience the unlimited, empowering process of learning to choose positively.

<u>Trust</u>

- Trust begins with listening to the intuition or gut level feeling—that little voice that we often ignore that shows up very fleetingly and subtly.

- Trust in yourself
- Trust in a Higher Power
- Trust in Humankind

Behaviors That Require Trust

- Acknowledgment and conscious or expressed gratitude
- Letting go of expectations of others
- Letting go of judgment and criticism
- Cleaning up incomplete agreements
- Listening to another's point of view
- Disentangling from negative relationships

The Trust Process

Answer the following questions as honestly as you can:

1. In what ways do you trust yourself?

   _____

   _____

   _____

2. How do you behave when you are operating from trust?

_____

_____

_____

3. How do you behave when trust is <u>not</u> present?

_____

_____

_____

You are still the same person in any given situation whether you choose to trust or not trust. Intuitively, trust is present within all of us, because trust is creative energy—pure and unscathed.

4. If you choose to trust, how will your experience change?

_____

_____

_____

Unlock Your Heart: Goal Setting from the Inside Out

5. In what areas of your life is trust missing?

   _____

   _____

   _____

6. Look at each area separately. Recall past experiences where a lack of trust hindered your progress.

   _____

   _____

   _____

7. Did you create the lack of trust, or did it come from someone else? _____

Recall as many similar experiences from the past as you can and notice the pattern. Spot who or what instilled the distrust in you. Try to remember the earliest time you experienced a lack of trust and see if you can pinpoint where you made an emotional decision regarding your ability to trust or be trusted. Write about the earliest experience and the decision you made.

_____

_____

The decision you made was probably not rational. When your emotions are involved, the decisions you make come from what you are feeling at the time. Your intellectual mind does not make the decision. It is formed in your subconscious mind. That is why the decision is usually not rational. The mind then functions from that irrational decision and justifies it.

The challenge is to notice your decision to trust or not to trust, acknowledge it, and choose to take charge of it. Try restating your lack of trust in positive, empowering language. Write out your positive decision statement.

_____

_____

When old decisions show up, simply repeat the new, empowering thought or idea regarding who you are *being* now. Each time the old decisions appear you can make a positive choice. This process allows the old patterns to shift and no longer create barriers to your progress.

Unlock Your Heart: Goal Setting from the Inside Out

Example

One client realized through this process that she did not trust adults. We looked into her experiences as a child and discovered why. She was orphaned as a baby and was raised by a number of foster parents. She spent a great deal of time being moved from one foster home to another. She often felt abandoned and found that she could not trust what adults would tell her. She decided at an early age that all adults could not be trusted. They were not available to love her, and she would always be alone. Naturally this subconscious decision caused her problems throughout her childhood and adult life. She was abandoned in relationships and ultimately found herself alone. While practicing the techniques in this process she discovered that she could alter that early childhood decision and create astounding results in her relationships with others and herself. She has since acquired many wonderful friends and a deep communication with her spiritual nature. She now declares on a regular basis, "I am lovable and am surrounded by joyous, loving people who contribute love to me and accept love from me unconditionally." It works for her because she has chosen to believe it. So she exudes a

Jane Ellen Davis

confidence with others that comes from her ability to be loving. Consequently, others respond in a loving way. In the earlier exercise, one of her core values is Expressing and Receiving Love unconditionally.

When an old decision shows up simply repeat the new, empowering thought or idea regarding who you are *being*. Now each time this happens, you can make a positive choice. This process allows that old pattern to shift and no longer create barriers to your progress.

Processes for Releasing Resentments, Completing Unhealthy Relationships, and Cleaning Up Incomplete Agreements

In order to move out of old beliefs and limiting thoughts, there are certain things that need to be handled. It is vital to let go of any resentment you are holding onto, regardless of the cause of the resentment. When you hold resentment, the energy and attention put into keeping it alive causes you to remain stuck. You cannot proceed or grow in a creative manner when resentments are present. Your attention gets fixed on the story connected to the resentment. Energy that could be used positively is wasted.

Unlock Your Heart: Goal Setting from the Inside Out

In order to let go of resentment, begin by recalling each resentment you are holding. Concentrate first on the most immediate resentments: those with family members, co-workers, employers, etc. No doubt the family resentments will be more long term. Look at each one individually and thoroughly.

Do the following processes for each resentment.

1) Notice who is involved and the facts surrounding the resentment. Try to stick to the facts and not the story behind them. What is likely to show up is that someone did not fulfill your expectation.

2) Notice what the expectation is or was. The important step now is to release the hurt feelings and disappointment you have attached to the failure of the other person to fulfill an expectation. Expectations you hold for another are often a setup for hurt feelings or disappointment. You cannot expect a specific behavior from another. This expectation puts the other person in a position of pressure and responsibility that can make that

person feel suffocated. This can be very damaging to a relationship.

3) Now look at what your responsibility to yourself was in that particular incident. How could you have behaved differently? Could you have communicated more clearly? The important issue here is to take personal responsibility for the role you played in the incident.

4) Recreate the facts in your mind so that you are approaching the occurrence without a preconceived expectation of the result. How would the incident have transpired if you had not had a particular expectation of the other person?

If it is possible to communicate with the individual(s) involved, forgiving the person and releasing the resentment can be quite healing. You will be amazed at the outcome.

If you are unable or unwilling to communicate with the person, or if it interferes in his or her life or causes turmoil, do it in your thoughts. Say what you need to say to let go of the resentment and allow the other person to get and receive what you are saying. Then tell yourself what you would want the other to say back to you (not what you think they would say). Then acknowledge that person's words and forgive any wrong you felt he or she did. Forgive yourself for any responsibility you had in the upset. This is perhaps the most important aspect of the exercise. Self-forgiveness allows the upset to clear up and it removes the possibility that you will repeat the same mistake. The cleansing process is complete when you declare your forgiveness. Do this process with each resentment. The benefit is the abundance of new energy available once the resentment is cleared. All resentment does is keep you stopped, immobilized and limited! Let it go, and release your need to be right, no matter how painful the hurt feelings are. Complete these as soon as possible and free up your creativity and joy.

<u>Example</u>

One client found he was carrying a heavy resentment regarding his ex-wife. He felt anger and sadness connected to their breakup. She was having an affair and ultimately left him. He came to me for some clarity and some relief from his upset. We spent some time examining the circumstance around the split and his resentments began surfacing. These feelings of anger and sadness were overwhelming him. We spent several sessions using the resentment techniques. The most profound cleansing came when he was able to communicate in a mock situation the expectations his ex-wife had not fulfilled. He also clearly understood the part he had played in not fulfilling her expectations. During his practice communication, he was able to forgive her and ask for her forgiveness. He no longer felt the need to make her wrong. He could let go of his hurt feelings and anger. Shortly after our sessions, his ex-wife, who lives in Europe, called him to beg his forgiveness and to express her appreciation for all he had attempted to provide for her during their marriage. One of his statements during our mock dialogue was having his wife say, "I am very sorry I caused you pain and suffering. You did your best to provide for me while we were together. I fully appreciate you now and want you to know that." You see he never spoke directly to her during our session. He spoke as though she were there. As you can see, the power of this process can sometimes be astounding. She received his loving forgiveness even though he did not talk to her directly. When she called he was then able to tell her he no longer resented her and had no hurt feelings. They are now good friends and actually e-mail each other occasionally.

Completing Unhealthy Relationships

Many times unresolved relationships keep you stuck. Perhaps an old work relationship, or a love relationship was terminated without a complete communication. Unresolved issues are present and keep your attention fixed or stuck. These issues may be controlling you without you even being aware of it. The outcome is that you will continue a pattern of similar problems attached to any new relationship, whether business or personal. The same mistakes keep showing up as long as you stay stuck.

Completion means the situation is okay as it is, and it is okay the way it is not. One is clear of any negative energy (thoughts) connected to the experience of the relationship. Completion begins with you noticing what took place when things began to fall apart. A visual deletion process is quite valuable here. It works much like a computer.

Completion Exercise

1. Imagine you are using a computer. Type the specific confusion or upset; notice the facts connected to the upset, then press delete.
2. Then type out the positive result you desire and press save.
3. Choose to believe the positive, release the negative. Press delete.

Withdrawing your energy from the negative belief removes its power.

Another easy exercise for dispensing unhealthy energy connected with a relationship is a process that gives you clarity on what really happened and how much of it was your responsibility.

Clarity Process

Let's say someone in a relationship has hurt your feelings. You are harboring resentment and anger and many other emotions connected with that person. Think about the action or lack of action taken by the person who caused the

Unlock Your Heart: Goal Setting from the Inside Out

hurt feelings. Think about what the person did, or did not do, that you are resenting. There will probably be several things that you will think of.

List Actions You Resented

1) _____

2) _____

3) _____

4) _____

_____

After your list is complete, notice what you did or did not do that might have contributed to the outcome of the resentment. Be honest here. When you begin to see the part you played, the responsibility for the outcome becomes yours as well as the other person's. This awareness causes a shift in your point of view regarding the hurt you experienced. Once you can acknowledge your part in the events, you will feel an amazing release of your pent-up emotions. You will be able to take responsibility for your role and you will feel less resentful. You must also be willing to forgive yourself for your role in the upset.

My Role

_____

_____

_____

Once you have done the Clarity Process it is unbelievably cleansing to contact the person and complete the communication. You will not blame that person any more. Sometimes it is not possible, or is not safe, to contact the person. But when it is, the emotional release and healing that transpires is awesome. The freedom it promotes is magical.

The beauty of expressing forgiveness, regardless of the destructive deeds done by the person you are forgiving, is freeing for both people. Learning to forgive and move on in peace is one of the greatest lessons you can experience.

Unlock Your Heart: Goal Setting from the Inside Out

Forgiveness allows you to create miracles in your daily life. It frees you up to welcome new, splendid relationships and become who you truly aspire to be.

Examining your personal truth is not always easy. Being truthful with others really has its roots in discovering what your personal truth is. This truth is inside all the values you hold dear. Learned behavior, family dynamics, background and upbringing all play an integral role in your understanding of truthfulness.

If your goal is to be authentic in all your actions, truth must be present. Personal honesty asks, "Who are you really being? What do you really want? How are you really feeling?"

When you take away all the shoulds, remove all the perceptions and suggestions from others, and get down to the gut level of personal self-worth and integrity, all the secrets, miscommunications, incomplete agreements, resentments and hurt feelings you hold in place by not telling the truth are diminished. Imagine freeing up all that energy now being consumed by past upsets and negativity.

We have been spending some time finding ways to unlock your heart and understand who you are as your values. We have discovered that your internal make-up is who you are naturally. Your Higher Self dwells in that natural state—devoid of any fear or distrust.

In order to free ourselves of upsets and fear, we must look at any thing we are withholding (not telling the truth about). Let's call these withholds, secrets. Jot down any secrets that immediately come to mind. Once you have them written down, read them again and notice what part you played in the circumstance connected to the secret. Tell the truth to yourself. This is where the fear will surface. Depending upon the seriousness of the secret, your concern about being found out will be quite evident. I invite you to embrace the fear—be with it—try it on—stand in it.

Let your fear share with you what it is afraid of. Words may actually form or you may just have a feeling. Let the fear speak. This fear is connected to your subconscious—the fear thinks it is protecting you. Somewhere in your early childhood, maybe even at birth, the false idea that your fear represents became a part of you. As the fear tells its story be gentle with yourself. Chances are, surrounding this secret, nobody ever has been. It is up to you to be there for yourself at this point. Do not suppress or ignore that fear or feeling of panic or concern. Once the fear has had the chance to express itself, your conscious awareness can acknowledge its existence. Acknowledge that you understand and send love to that voice that is sharing the fear. Let it know you are in charge and are choosing to handle the situation. This comforts that fearfulness and allows you to shift your attitude and your perception of what might happen if you were truthful. Many times just doing this exercise eliminates much of the burden you have been carrying. The energy around the situation disperses and you have clarity on what the best method is for dealing with it.

Fear definitely stops progress. Notice the fear, let it speak, listen to it, validate it and acknowledge it for wanting to protect you. Reassure your fear that you are in control and are choosing to take over. Love it; honor it—set it free to be. Then recreate the scenario you believe is your personal purpose and set your creative beliefs in motion and *be* those beliefs. That's it! If you can trust those guidelines and be those natural talents you can create miracles because who you are naturally is a miracle. Awesome, isn't it?

Jane Ellen Davis

Session Three

<u>Visualize: Being/Doing/Having</u>

In Session Three you will be writing and visualizing the new way of *being* that you have been bringing to the surface in Sessions One and Two. Based on what you have already learned in the first two sessions, you know now that you must *be* before you can do anything. As Session One pointed out, when you notice who you are *being* in each moment, it is out of that *beingness* that *doing* takes shape. If you are *being* authentic, behaving in a manner that exemplifies your personal truth, the *doingness* that accompanies the exemplification is effortless. It flows, the activity occurs quite spontaneously, in perfect harmony. The result is clarity, order, completion, and a beneficial outcome (a result that benefits you and makes a contribution to others).

It is important here to understand the distinction between *being, doing* and *having.* In the Western way of learning, we have been taught that in order to be productive, we must begin with doing, and be focused on

Unlock Your Heart: Goal Setting from the Inside Out

the result of the doing. The Western belief follows a Do, Be, Have order. I am suggesting a Be, Do, Have order. When you begin with who you are *being,* you are clearly focused on your inner resources and your production will reflect that focus. The doing just evolves naturally. The outcome of your actions evolving from your inner resources will be what you have. That outcome will far exceed any expectation you had.

If you have truly honored your natural way of *being,* whatever you are doing will be appropriate and focused so that the outcome (what you have) as a result will be perfect. The key in learning to behave this way is to trust the outcome and **release any attachment to it**. Don't attempt to manipulate the results. By holding on to your expectations of the outcome, you block the very energy that could produce an enhanced outcome. Nothing needs to be forced. The entire process appears to just evolve without glitches or pitfalls. When you trust your natural ability and become one with it, a Higher Consciousness is in charge of the outcome you need and want, even though the final outcome may not appear to be the goal you outlined. It may differ from your original goal, but when you really examine it, you will appreciate that it is a refined, precise version of your goal, with a beneficial outcome that will contribute even more to you. Most likely others will benefit as well. *Being* authentic gives you the opportunity to expand your circle of influence within your immediate environment, your community and the world.

A good test is to write out a current goal as though it has already happened and begin noticing what kind of energy you will need to contribute to create that goal. If you are able to utilize your natural abilities and be actively calm in pursuing the goal, you are *on purpose* with who you are *being.* If you feel uncomfortable, or overly stressed in your action steps, re-evaluate the goal. Something within it will show up as inauthentic or off purpose. Something does not line up with your basic values or your highest desires for truth. Restructure the goal so it serves your natural ability, and the stress and effort attached to the action will disappear.

Example

As one of her real estate goals, Pat wrote, "I have increased my income by $20,000 and my listings by 20%."

Unlock Your Heart: Goal Setting from the Inside Out

Pat experienced a great deal of stress and upset as a result of attempting to achieve this goal. As she examined her goal she discovered that she had neglected to include her three core values of Love, Adventure and Beauty.

Her restructured goal:

> "By focusing my attention on the needs and wants of my clients and genuinely caring about their satisfaction and selecting properties that suit them, I have increased my income by $20,000 and my listings by 20%."

What she discovered, as a result of her restructured goal, was that her energy level increased dramatically. She was able to organize her day with less stress. Her communication with her clients improved because she was thoughtfully listening to their needs. She made a genuine effort to honor their desires for beauty and comfort. Within her office, she noticed other agents responding more positively to her. Several even asked her what she was doing differently. So, she not only improved her relationship with her job, she created a positive change in the entire work environment.

When your goal is aligned with your core values, skills and talents, you will experience enthusiasm and well-being. Your actions for supporting the goal will be fueled by the passion that fully exemplifies who you really are.

The key in all of this is to trust the outcome to the Divine, your Creative Source. You must be willing to surrender any attachment to the outcome. Your only focus ultimately is on *being* your passion in each precious moment. This passion is definitely fueling any doingness and what you will have in any given moment is the joy of *being* your passion.

Now that you have some clarity on your life purpose (why you are here, what your natural ability and longing beckon you to be and do), it is time to get those creative juices flowing. The choreography begins now—allow yourself to quiet down and listen within. Really own the purpose you just claimed. It is who you are, it is God's gift to you and your gift to God is to own that purpose and create it as your life. Some of you may prefer to think of

Unlock Your Heart: Goal Setting from the Inside Out

your natural gifts and talents as pure Creative Energy, or Universal Consciousness. Use whatever reference compliments your personal beliefs. For some, this is so new and frightening—just trust the process and continue with whatever has come up for you.

Whatever level of understanding you are currently experiencing is the perfect level. No one is judging you or your purpose. There is no right or wrong in these exercises, just the opportunity to move out of a limited comfort zone into a brilliant experience of the richness of your spirit. The spirit that is your essence is waiting within to be rediscovered and manifested now.

Creating Scenarios

You are going to begin creating scenarios describing your personal desires. In the next exercise the core values you identified in Session One are going to be incorporated into a series of scenes that best depict the way you would like your life to be. The descriptions of each scene will be based on you being the very best you can be by following your values.

Jane Ellen Davis

You will be concentrating on the three major core values you selected. You are going to be using your imagination, envisioning yourself at your best. Think about the way you would behave. Let your mind and your heart blend as you picture what your actions would be like if you demonstrated your values. Describe the passion and the excitement that would come from you. Imagine all the amazing choices and experiences you could have as that empowered person. It is important for you to believe that you have always possessed those natural abilities.

As you read through Pat's example, notice her clear description of who she is at her best. You can see that she really believes what she is describing is possible.

Example

Remember Pat's three core values are Adventure, Beauty and Love.

"Being the most I can be as Adventure, I am high-energy while being with loved ones out in nature, i.e., going down the Grand Canyon on the Colorado River. It's the sharing of the adventure—being thrilled—being totally

Unlock Your Heart: Goal Setting from the Inside Out

in the moment—FUN! The who I am is high-energy, fast paced activity—a 'Yes, we did it'!"

Notice the excitement within her scenario. You can feel that she is *being* that high-energy she describes. You can almost hear her shout "Yes" as she finishes riding the rapids on the river. She truly is *being* Adventure at its best.

In her scenario about Love she states, "Unconditionally loving and accepting people as who they are. Being judgment free. Receiving love from all sources available. Generating love from a heartfelt, wholesome space without expectations."

Begin now by writing a scenario of who you are as each of your three core values—being the best that you can be. I encourage you to take this exercise very seriously. This is the way you are going to unlock all those longings that lie below the surface and that are usually quite timid about showing up.

Jane Ellen Davis

SCENARIO ONE: MY CORE VALUE: _____
DESCRIPTION _____

_____

_____

_____

_____

_____

_____

SCENARIO ONE: MY CORE VALUE: _____
DESCRIPTION _____

_____

_____

_____

_____

_____

_____

Unlock Your Heart: Goal Setting from the Inside Out

SCENARIO ONE: MY CORE VALUE: _____
DESCRIPTION _____

_____

_____

_____

_____

_____

_____

After you have completed each of your scenarios, go back and read what you have written. Really allow the words to sink in. Get how energizing and fulfilling your descriptions are. You just described yourself at your best, giving and receiving in a jubilant way. Look over each description and notice what is amazing. What surprises you? What takes your breath away?

Remember the examples of my own three core values:

Unconditional Love, Creative Self-expression and Freedom.

Jane Ellen Davis

EXAMPLE

My core value of Unconditional Love means:

1) Understanding and accepting all people without judgment.
2) Noticing the brilliance of each precious being, acknowledging everyone for his or her natural creativity.
3) Energizing and being energized.
4) Receiving as well as giving joyously.
5) Being willing to be deeply intimate and share myself fully.

By being the most I can be as Unconditional Love, I openly rejoice in each dear one I encounter. I listen for and notice the longing and the truth spoken by each, even when it is hidden beneath complaints and barriers. I inspire each one to embrace their natural greatness and believe in themselves. I encourage, motivate and educate each one on ways to renew creative energy and produce whatever is his or her heart's desire. I celebrate the wonder of the Universe

Unlock Your Heart: Goal Setting from the Inside Out

with all I touch. Who I am *being* enlightens who you are becoming!

As I read through what I wrote, I notice what is amazing, surprising and takes my breath away. First of all, the idea of sharing myself on my most intimate level without fear and with complete trust—that is amazing! Receiving expressions of love, with no strings attached, no expectations of who I am supposed to be, no judgment! That is surprising! Experiencing Love flowing to me from all aspects of my life takes my breath away. I am in bliss when I see this scenario in all its splendor. When I believe in the possibility of this really happening, I am in awe.

Once you have gone through each of your three scenarios you will notice a personal passionate purpose that flows from one scenario to another. Remember your purpose is what drives you; it is why you do what you do; it is a deep belief in yourself; it is your creative talent.

My passionate purpose in the scenario I demonstrated for you is to be fully present in a non-judgmental way—understanding, inspiring, and guiding all people to be their natural creativity. That purpose will flow through all my scenarios because it is what I do best naturally. I do not have to work at it. When I am trusting myself those qualities of inspiration and guidance just occur naturally. I am so grateful that I have been able to create a career that allows me to generate that natural gift **I stand for each one of you discovering your natural gifts and creating ways to live that gift on a daily basis.**

Unlock Your Heart: Goal Setting from the Inside Out

Session Four

<u>Creating Realms</u>

By now you have clarity on who you desire to be in order to have the doing flow naturally. Session Four will guide you in identifying each aspect of your life in a bold, new way. All the areas of your life, your career, your family relationships, social relationships, spiritual life, and any other areas you wish to identify will be placed in a Realm. The dictionary defines a Realm as a kingdom, a region; sphere; area (the Realm of thought). These Realms will reflect your deepest values. Each Realm will have specific goals to keep you focused on your values and purpose. The goals you set here are based upon the scenarios you created in Session Three. Within those scenarios lies the essence of who you are. The talents that are uniquely yours hold all the secrets to an abundant and joyful lifestyle. Begin by rereading the first scenario you created. Underline key words and phrases that best describe your natural abilities and intrinsic values. As you do this for each scenario, a pattern will probably develop. You will see how one passionate purpose is linked with each scenario. Since you worked on this in Session One, you should be feeling more familiar with your purpose by now. Knowing and owning your purpose, that underlying energy that fuels your personal desires for fulfillment, keeps you focused. That purpose provides your guideline for measuring your progress at any given time. Within that purpose is a very deep, powerful intention. You know what you want and you form your thoughts to produce what you want. That is strong intention. It is passionate and it is so intrinsic to your nature that you engage all your creative energy into demonstrating that intention. Your determined focus generates that intention out into all you are *being.* If you are off purpose things begin to break down—you will get stopped, you won't get cooperation from others, your successes will dwindle. When this occurs it is definitely time for a purpose check-up. Ask yourself, "Where am I off purpose?" Take stock of each aspect of your life and it will surely be apparent where you have strayed. Once you identify the area lacking purpose, you can choose to regroup and correct the situation by redefining your purpose and adjusting who you are *being* in that situation.

Unlock Your Heart: Goal Setting from the Inside Out

It generally will not be someone else causing the problem, even though it may seem that way initially. Once you <u>really</u> tell the truth to yourself about your responsibility in the situation, you can create the necessary energy to get back to purposeful activity.

Once you have studied your first scenario and have identified the purpose that sets your heart pumping and excites you, you are ready to begin developing concrete, measurable goals designed to promote that purpose. How are you going to actualize the highest level of joy and satisfaction that scenario speaks of? Look again at your scenario. What is the very first step you must take to start developing reality within your ideal scene? Where can you begin to take charge of choosing to live this way? It may be a baby step, but it is a beginning. It is the commitment to choosing and taking action that starts the creative energy flowing. Without the commitment and the acknowledgment that you do have a choice, that brilliant scenario will probably not transpire. Remember, this is about who you are in all your natural, God-given ability and talent.

Jane Ellen Davis

So the requirement here is that you can actually believe in the possibility of your scenario coming true. If you see it as a pipe dream, it will probably be just that.

The three scenarios you created are the roots of all of your Realms. Remember your Realms are the areas of your life: your career or job, your relationships with family, friends, a husband/wife or significant other, your spiritual beliefs, your relationship with yourself physically, mentally, and emotionally, etc. Each scenario is a significant aspect of your Realms. Those core values you exemplified in your scenarios also exist in your Realms.

The goals, or intentions, that you create based on your scenarios, will be the energy that is connected to creating wonderful possibilities in each Realm.

As you look over your scenarios, begin connecting each one to your Realms. Notice where the energy you described in the scenarios can easily be applied to each Realm to start making a difference in the way you behave in each aspect of your life. Once you consciously choose to begin behaving in the manner you described, you will experience a difference in the quality of your life. This is because you have taken over as the choreographer and the director of how you are going to give and receive. You are owning those core values, you are speaking differently, you are behaving differently, you are listening to others differently, you are receiving more honest, open communication from those you interact with on a daily basis. You have let go of expectations of others, you no longer expect someone to do or be a certain way with you. You love them and accept whatever they have to offer without judgment. You are showing up without a hidden agenda. That means you are not already pre-judging how they should behave or what they should do for you. It means you intend for each of you to benefit from your interaction.

Now we are ready to begin creating a Realm for each aspect of your life: career/job, social relationships, family relationships, spiritual, physical, mental, emotional, financial, etc. Rather than have you just label each Realm by these basic terms, I am suggesting you go deeper and get to the heart of each of these areas. When you trust yourself to look inside of each area and discover where those core values we have been working with surface, you are becoming more real and honoring your natural creativity.

Jane Ellen Davis

You are ready to go beyond categorizing your life in the basic way.

Begin by choosing an area: let's say your career or job. Write a brief description of your career or job. As you describe it, do so from the values you discovered and used in your scenarios. You are describing a deeper level of what it is you do. You are describing the motivation within your work. If you are currently in a job or career that you do not like, or doesn't suit who you have discovered you are as your values, write about a career that you would enjoy. Go ahead and make it up for now.

For example: my career is absolutely what I want to do and it is fulfilling for me because I get to be what I am creatively gifted to be. So I am choosing to call my Career Realm "Total Fulfillment" because for me it is. The greatest joy of my career is in Life Choreography Network (the name of my business). It provides me with the opportunity to use my personal freedom to choose, to express myself creatively and to practice demonstrating Unconditional Love on all levels. I guide, motivate, inspire, teach, coach, listen, and flow love to all my clients. I do one-on-one guidance; I give instructional workshops that I

Unlock Your Heart: Goal Setting from the Inside Out

call Playgrounds in all areas of Personal Growth; I do Spiritual Counseling; I hold retreats for self-discovery and increased awareness; I lecture and write. The beauty and greatness of each client emerges from the processes we do together. It is joyous and fulfilling to be the catalyst for each one's growth. As you can see, I wrote from a powerful place, acknowledging my part in what transpires with my clients. I described the best of who I am. This is the method I want you to try on as you describe your career.

The next step after you write a description is to answer the following questions. What is at this Realm's core? What is it that makes the Realm unique and special? How does the energy within the Realm operate? Who are you within the Realm?

Example: What is at this Realm's core? That means deep inside of the actions and responsibilities connected with what you do, there is a motivation and strong desire to create something extraordinary. In my description, what is at the core is my desire to be real. My desire is to show up moment to moment in an authentic manner that inspires others to drop their barriers and embrace their natural creativity and all the gifts they brought into this life experience. Understanding the kind of work I do, you can imagine how vitally important it is for me to be authentic when I serve my clients.

Next question: What is it that makes the Realm unique or special for me? It is a sense of knowing when to listen, when to speak, when to honor, when to love and cry, when to rejoice and celebrate, when to acknowledge, when to challenge, when to be silent and wait. It is fully expressing Spirit.

Next question: How does the energy within the Realm operate? There is no hesitation, no mental chatter, no judgment, no expectation, no forcing the outcome, no attachment to a result. It is fully accepting and honoring and expressing joy. It operates cleanly and clearly.

Next question: Who am I within the Realm? I am the catalyst. I hold the space for true creativity to manifest itself in each person I work with. I am free from judgment and I listen for the passion spoken. I acknowledge, I encourage, I challenge greatness. I inspire others to manifest exquisite abundance and prosperity in their lives.

I will use Darlene's example of her career Realm because she is not particularly happy with her job. She would like to create something better. She loves to travel and she has wonderful teaching skills. She decided to create a career Realm that would allow her to incorporate her love of travel. Even though this particular job has not manifested, she is willing to create the possibility.

<u>Darlene's Career Realm-Natural Teacher</u>

Description of Realm

"I travel and give information to those I travel with (history, cultural information). I lead tours of interesting, offbeat places. Small groups. Tours are based on a creative approach. Fun, eccentric, unique. I am a guide—not a leader. I help others to look at the world in a different way. 'Would you like to stay in a Navajo Hogan? How about a visit to a home in the desert carved from a rock? Everything you've ever wanted to know about turtles? That too.' Sometimes, visits to spiritual places with shaman elders. Sometimes lectures on former trips."

Jane Ellen Davis

What is at the core of this Realm?

"The essence of this work is creativity. That is its core."

What makes this Realm unique or special?

"I am teaching others about the world around them. Helping them to see the great beauty of the world. Sharing their amazement about that beauty. Giving them a different perspective from which to view their regular lives. The joy and cultural knowledge they derive gives me a sense of pleasure and fulfillment."

How does the energy within the Realm operate?

"The enthusiasm I generate is catching. All those who travel with me are equally excited and eager to experience meeting people from other cultures. There is an air of fun and adventure. Everyone participates and shares in the joy of seeing new places."

Who am I within the Realm?

"I point the way. I map out our journeys. I am the storyteller, the guide, the one who motivates the group. I enlist others in assisting me with the organizational tasks. Everyone catches my enthusiasm."

As you can see, Darlene was able to touch the vibrancy of her passion about travel. She found a way to make it a very important part of her life. Now she will have more clarity on what it is she really wants. She will begin to find ways to channel her energy toward creating this Realm.

The second Realm I created for myself I called Astounding Relationships. I wanted this Realm to represent my desire to experience a loving relationship with a wonderful man. As I was creating this Realm, I discovered much more than a personal relationship with a man. The Realm took on a much higher purpose then my own happiness in a relationship.

Jane Ellen Davis

My Relationship Realm-Astounding Relationships

Example of the Realm

Sharing: giving and receiving passion and understanding. A loving, intimate man sharing with me on all levels. Awesome communication, a sharing based in trust and intimacy—authentic and full of a rich integrity and passion. A belief in the power of magic, dreams and personal magnificence, far beyond the ordinary—extraordinary, outrageous and fully self-expressed. Always up to something adventurous and stimulating—totally believing in synchronicity and synergy. Creating a difference globally-connecting other cultures and experiencing their passion for who they are at their best.

What is at the core of this Realm?

Passion is the core—smoldering, creative joy—new ways to create abundance for all—honoring each culture and each individual for their personal contribution—prosperity, however that is real for each person—

inspiration and reassurance that who they are is awesome and powerful, and that they truly make a difference.

What makes this Realm unique or special?

It is the opportunity to create possibility—to go beyond the ordinary and stand for astounding achievement and contribution by creating food for all, shelter for all, magnificence for each human being—fully experiencing their personal greatness.

How does the energy within the Realm operate?

The energy is a coming together to collectively escalate the richness of the human experience so that all are being who they were created to be in their own culture. Families heal old wounds and embrace each other. Communities listen and honor all needs. Countries operate with integrity and honor. All people are fed, clothed and sheltered—each contributing the talent and gifts they are able to manifest from their personal creativity. The world vibrates with astounding, loving energy—there is agreement and affinity among all nations and the Universe rejoices—The Angels sing!

Who am I within the Realm?

I am the visionary. I represent the eyes, the ears and the heart of the world—viewing all as God's creation. I stand for this incredible truth and hold it in my thoughts. I am encouragement and enthusiasm for this wonderful vision.

Unlock Your Heart: Goal Setting from the Inside Out

Create A Realm for Each Area of Your Life

Realm-Name it: _____

Describe it: _____

_____

_____

_____

_____

_____

1) What is at the core of the Realm?

_____

_____

_____

_____

2) What makes this Realm unique or special?

_____

_____

_____

_____

3) How does the energy within the Realm operate?

_____

_____

_____

_____

4) Who am I within the Realm?

_____

_____

_____

_____

_____

_____

<u>Note</u>: You may want to have a separate Realm for family and friends, within your relationship descriptions—remember you are creating this. Your Realms may be different than these examples. Use your own words to describe your life aspects.

Unlock Your Heart: Goal Setting from the Inside Out

Realm-Name it: _____

Describe it: _____

1) What is at the core of the Realm?

2) What makes this Realm unique or special?

3) How does the energy within the Realm operate?

4) Who am I within the Realm?

Unlock Your Heart: Goal Setting from the Inside Out

Create A Realm for Each Area of Your Life

Realm-Name it: _____

_____

Describe it: _____

_____

_____

_____

_____

_____

1) What is at the core of the Realm?

_____

_____

_____

_____

2) What makes this Realm unique or special?

_____

_____

_____

_____

_____

3) How does the energy within the Realm operate?

4) Who am I within the Realm?

Unlock Your Heart: Goal Setting from the Inside Out

Create A Realm for Each Area of Your Life

Realm-Name it: _____

_____

Describe it: _____

_____

_____

_____

_____

_____

1) **What is at the core of the Realm?**

_____

_____

_____

_____

_____

2) **What makes this Realm unique or special?**

_____

_____

_____

_____

_____

3) How does the energy within the Realm operate?

4) Who am I within the Realm?

<u>**Continue this process for any additional Realms you want to create**</u>.

Once you have designed each Realm, take a brief break. This is intense work you have been doing. Take a minute to be proud of what you have accomplished! Read over your

Unlock Your Heart: Goal Setting from the Inside Out

Realms several times and absorb what you have described. You are creating your astounding future. You are taking charge and manifesting breakthroughs even as you begin reading what you wrote. Those words, those descriptions of who you really are, already have power. Once you begin owning them, your energy will shift.

In Session Five you will be taking the next step creating goals to accompany those exciting Realms you are now claiming.

Session Five

Goals as Purposeful Intentions

The next step you will be taking is to create goals to accompany those exciting Realms you are now claiming. Each Realm you have designed and envisioned as real and already happening, depicts you at your best. The goals you outline are meant to enhance the opportunities that will manifest to have those Realms become a reality. We will discuss the definition here to be sure you have clarity on the method of goal setting being introduced.

Goals—The Definition: purposeful intentions and possibilities specifically stated on paper, affirmed visually, actively pursued, with no attachment to the outcome. Purposeful intentions indicate that whatever action is applied is going to line up with your purpose. You intend to remain clearly focused and purposeful. The more focused and intent you are on contributing positive energy when you take action, the greater the opportunity for success will be. Your intention is the powerful tool. Intention and commitment are linked in all the actions that

Unlock Your Heart: Goal Setting from the Inside Out

take place from who you are *being*. The sessions you have been studying are designed to put you in touch with your deepest intentions. Those purposeful desires are your goals.

Possibilities/opportunities that are created from deep intention are far beyond what is commonly experienced within a comfort zone. It is important to write out goals and state them as specifically as possible to give them the opportunity to be extremely powerful. Once the goals are written out, allow yourself to visualize them completed in all their splendor. Strongly affirm them and see them in your mind's eye. The next aspect of the definition is to actively pursue the goal and to release any attachment to the outcome.

For most of us, that definition works and sounds right until the last statement. The logical mind says why would I not want to be attached to the outcome? Isn't the outcome the reason I am pursuing the goal? The answer is based on a metaphysical principle founded on trust. Yes, you are pursuing a goal to experience a wonderful result. However, releasing your attachment to the outcome allows a far more beneficial and extraordinary result to transpire. When you are so attached to the intended result, you hinder the possibilities that could evolve. In an attempt to force or control the outcome you are in a sense holding it back. Think about the earlier conversation about trust. If you can learn to trust that your actions are based on your empowered beingness, the resulting benefits can be far more astounding then you ever imagined. So, experiment with letting go of any feeling of forcing or manipulating your goals. Be the best you can be, actively calm and calmly active as you become your intentions. Remember that creative energy is what will mobilize you and manifests your desires. That creative juice is what fuels all your activities connected to achieving your goals.

Those of you who have been conventional goal setters for years will find this extremely challenging. So much of the past instruction regarding goals has been emphasizing the doing of the goal. You will still be involved in doing something, but the energy around that doing is based on the inner resource of your pure creativity. Once you get a taste of what that produces, you will understand and trust this process. It will become easier each time you apply these principles.

Unlock Your Heart: Goal Setting from the Inside Out

It is time to try out creating goals to accompany your Realms. Begin with the Realm you are most passionate about. This is probably the Realm where your dreams of making a difference are located. The Realm that says if only things were different, I would do this. Choose to begin with a powerful Realm.

Read over what you wrote in your description of that Realm. Visualize yourself *being* the empowered person you described. See all the aspects you wrote about.

Ask yourself, where can I begin to apply my intentions to be the energy that will begin the process? Make some notes regarding the thoughts and ideas that surface at this point.

_____

_____

_____

_____

_____

_____

Notice if those ideas are in balance with your purpose and values. If they are, then begin creating those ideas into more purposeful intentions. The actions you apply will set the goal in motion.

Pat wrote a beautiful Relationship Realm in which she described her ideal of togetherness with a wonderful man. She entitled her Realm "Rich, Intimate Relationship": powerful, passionate partnership, able to express freely, exciting, loving, caring, open, like-minded and different, mischievous, playful, *being* beautiful together, willingness to not know, true communication, genuine love, great sense of humor, traveling through life as a wonderful adventure. Intimacy and richness and passion are fully present. It is the spice of life, the creation of a new entity combining 'we two'. It operates with the vitality and exuberance generated by our coming and being together. I am a goddess, a lover, an enchantress, an intelligent, fun-loving partner whose love and commitment are boundless.

That sounds like an awesome relationship, doesn't it? Let's look at some of the goals she created to support that Realm/Vision. Her goals are stated as purposeful intentions. She states them as if they are already taking place.

Pat's Goals

I am purposely expressing myself in a joyous manner when I am meeting men at social gatherings and business-oriented functions. I am spontaneously listening and enjoying what they have to share.

I am taking an active part in community service and organizations where like-minded men will be present.

I am attending lectures and seminars on creating awesome relationships and communicating from compassion and honor.

Once Pat has committed to contributing the energy needed to begin actively participating, she will be involved because she is anxious to demonstrate her desire for a rich, intimate relationship. There will be joy and enthusiasm coming from her as she involves herself in these chosen activities. She is honoring herself and her values and, because she will be those values when she participates, men will be automatically attracted to her by her enthusiasm. The particular type of man she seeks will be most likely to respond to her.

Once she has her goals firmly stated on paper and has visualized herself in these situations with focused intention, she is ready to apply the action plan to accompany these intentions. Session Six will guide you into this aspect of your master plan.

Let's review Darlene's career Realm: Natural Teacher. Her Realm describes the energy and joy she derives from creating travel adventures and being a guide for others. As she began to consider her purposeful intentions she realized the importance of helping others to look at the world in a more profound way. Since she is not already actively participating in group travel excursions, her goals are going to focus on beginning to create her Realm.

Darlene's Goals

I am researching several Pueblos in Arizona and New Mexico. I am creating a trip for a small group of amateur photographers to visit several Pueblos.

I am interviewing with a local travel agency to sponsor me as a tour guide on local day trips to gain experience and build a clientele.

I am writing articles on the various trips I have taken in the past and am including photos. I am submitting these articles to the several newspapers and travel magazines.

Unlock Your Heart: Goal Setting from the Inside Out

As you can see, Darlene focused on starting to generate actions that will allow her Realm to become a reality. The goals she outlined will keep her in line with her purpose and she will easily stay on target because she is clear regarding her intentions.

To begin your goal setting process, decide which Realm you are most passionate about. Read over what you wrote in your description of that Realm. Create goals that will assist you in upholding your Realm. Your goals reflect your purposeful intentions. What exactly do you intend to create?

Remember to write your goals as if they have already happened or are in progress.

Goals to Accompany My Realms

(Continue this process with each of your Realms.)

Name of Realm: _____

Goals: _____

_____

Jane Ellen Davis

Name of Realm: _____

Goals: _____

_____

_____

_____

_____

_____

Name of Realm: _____

Goals: _____

_____

_____

_____

_____

_____

Name of Realm: _____

Goals:_____

_____

_____

_____

_____

Unlock Your Heart: Goal Setting from the Inside Out

Now that you have goals written for each of your Realms, you are ready to proceed to Session Six. You will learn how to create a project to support your Realm. The projects are designed to organize your plan of action. As you define your purpose within each project, you will gain clarity and begin taking responsibility for your time, energy and resources. Even if you have only written goals for one or two of your Realms, proceed to Session Six and follow the exercises presented. Once you gain clarity on the actions you must generate, you will have greater enthusiasm regarding all your Realms. The more real your intentions and passionate values become, the urgency you feel to make some positive choices and changes will grow and energize you.

Session Six

Creating A Master Plan
Actualizing Being, Doing and Having

In Session Five you worked with your scenarios and Realms and formed goals that contribute to the best possible outcome for each Realm. Your scenarios describe who you are when you are *being* your core values. Your Realms represent all the aspects of your life. The goals you created are intentions that support your deepest desires. Now comes the fun part—applying those goals to a plan that will guide and assist you in the action necessary to manifest those astounding opportunities you have envisioned.

The ultimate goal is to be present moment-to-moment actualizing your world as the most profound possibility. You are way beyond a quiet comfort zone existence. You are stretching with your innate sense of creative intelligence. The steps in each session have prepared you for who you are when you are at your best. You know now how you behave when you are flowing from your creative energy. When you are there, in that easy, carefree way of *being*, you are demonstrating your intentions. You have graduated from the ordinary to the extraordinary simply by choosing to become that special something that you have always known existed within you. You have tapped into your personal natural resource. What an awesome experience!

To excite and energize you in pursuing this process here are some examples from clients. Loree and Pat are in their natural resource mode moment to moment more often than in their " less than" identity. They are there because they believe in themselves as the possibility of manifesting their unlimited resource of powerful energy. They trust and know this is possible. They state their desires for the betterment of all mankind and they are willing to stand up for those desires. They empower the opportunity for those incredible happenings to become a reality. They see the opportunity—void of doubt and fear and they are willing to release their personal attachment to the outcome.

Loree came to me at a very low point in her life. She had been very successful as a clothing designer, living and working in New York. She missed her family and decided to return to Southern California. She took a job designing with a small company and was very unhappy with the people within the company. She resigned from her position with them and took a job as a waitress. When she finally sought my help, she was in a very heavy depression and felt she had completely lost touch with her life purpose (her natural creative ability as a designer). We spent some time looking into old belief systems and patterns from her past that were keeping her stuck and in much pain. We did processes similar to the ones presented in this text and she began to release old emotional baggage and reclaim her natural talents and belief in her personal, God-given gifts. She released resentments she held in place, she began communicating from love and joy, she trusted her inner strength and her life began to change. Her relationships no longer suffered, the perfect job showed up for her and she is now living a life she loves in San Francisco, earning a six-figure income. Her enthusiasm for life is attracting the caliber of people she longed for and she is utilizing her natural creativity on a daily basis.

The key factor here is her willingness to take charge of shifting her outlook and her consciousness. Without her

Unlock Your Heart: Goal Setting from the Inside Out

commitment to choosing a joy-filled life, it would not have happened. The people and experiences in her past did not change; her attachment to them shifted and she chose to view them differently. She adopted an attitude of gratitude and flowed love. It worked!

In this session all the preparation you have done is gathered up and the practical application of your committed intentions is assembled in a master plan.

In order to learn to have the vision to dream up a project or plan that excites you and utilizes your natural gifts and values, you need to know how to keep yourself focused on your vision. In other words, you must stay grounded with your intention. You own it, and believe in the possibility that it can happen. You visualize it as complete. You take a firm stand and you begin applying the energy to cause it to actualize. The grounding exercise will assist you in learning to create intense focus.

GROUNDING EXERCISE

The purpose of this exercise is to present a method that guides you to plant yourself in your heart consciousness. This exercise trains you to do your inner work. It assists

Jane Ellen Davis

you in developing an inner-communication with clarity and complete understanding. It focuses you and guides you in owning and demonstrating your greatness. It grounds you in *being* your passionate purpose.

Training ourselves to listen to internal longing takes practice. Most of us were not taught to pay attention to our deepest desire—the pearl within. Once we begin truly listening, we can experience what is being expressed within. Passionate self-expression propels us into creative action. (Read that line again and let it really sink in.)

See if you can answer the following questions as truthfully as possible. Repeat the questions several times until you know you are <u>really</u> telling the truth. You will know when you have tapped into that passionate place. Your energy will soar, your adrenaline will flow and you will automatically begin *being* that passion.

1. What is your passion (the pearl within)?

_____

_____

_____

_____

Unlock Your Heart: Goal Setting from the Inside Out

2. What do you want for yourself?

_____

_____

_____

_____

3. What do you want *from* yourself?

_____

_____

_____

_____

4. What do you want for another?

_____

_____

_____

_____

5. What are you willing to give up in order to get what you want?

_____

_____

Jane Ellen Davis

_____

_____

6. How can you serve the greater good?

_____

_____

_____

_____

7. What is the benefit?

_____

_____

_____

_____

8. How would your life experience improve?

_____

_____

_____

_____

Unlock Your Heart: Goal Setting from the Inside Out

Once you can honestly answer these questions and you begin to demonstrate them in your daily experience, a definite shift will occur. Your actions will assume that new posture of self-confidence, ease and grace. Your affect on others will shift. People will wake up around you. They will listen when you speak. They will enroll in your enthusiasm and embrace your ideas. When you consciously choose to demonstrate your natural talents moment to moment, your experience of the world will be different. The truth is, the world will not change, your view of it will. Your contribution elevates the vibration and you will experience a fulfilling life because of who you are *being.*

The greatest shift others will see is your aliveness. You show-up with more clarity, you are focused and empowered and they can feel your presence. Even if you do not consider yourself a leader, people will begin to respond to you as if you are. Your actions will be so naturally dynamic and spontaneous, free of doubt or hesitation, they will automatically respond favorably to your ideas.

Jane Ellen Davis

As you begin to actualize your personal truth, with each purposeful activity, state the ground upon which you stand. Who are you grounded in being? Read the example of the youth organization project in the next paragraph. If you had created the intention of a support network of adults and youth spending time together one-to-one, you would state that you were grounded (stand for firmly) in being the energy it takes to launch that project. You would act accordingly, *being* and doing whatever it takes to get the project underway. You would continue to be grounded in the belief that the project will indeed happen with or without you.

To give you an example of what I mean by standing for something far greater than what currently appears to be taking place, let's consider the following. Let's say you volunteer for a youth organization. You notice there is a need for a one-on-one adult/youth relationship program. You decide to create the foundation for that program in the form of a project. You design the ultimate description of your project as if it were already complete. You share your design with the powerful decision makers within the organization. It may seem, at first, impossible—perhaps due to lack of funding, community support, etc., but you continue to stand for the possibility that it will happen. You envision it in place, working successfully. You speak about it with assurance and enthusiasm. Before you know it, others will be enrolled in your vision. You will have supplied the belief that it is possible. Your energy will have created the opportunity. Once it is embraced by others and begins to manifest, your relationship to it shifts. You must be willing to let it go and trust the outcome will benefit all. It is no longer yours. This is the beauty of powerful vision. It expands to include all, you ultimately are just one of many contributors. The amazing result for you will be to enjoy the happiness and growth the children receive. This is no longer about you.

Once you begin to be all you are naturally and create from that space, the difference you make can be astounding. But it is not about you.

To begin creating your master plan take each Realm and think of it more like a project. A project involves your purpose and goals. When your Realm is formulated as a project, it is much easier to believe it really can happen. All of the action steps required to mobilize your Realm can be assembled within projects. Your most profound intentions become the meat of the project. Using a project approach allows you to stay focused and manage your time and energy in an orderly fashion. Creating projects for actualizing your realms allows you to remain on purpose, fulfilling your deepest intentions.

Check on your purpose within the Realm (why is the Realm significant and desirable?) Using your most passionate Realm (the one you identify with above all others) begin describing your project.

EXAMPLE: In Session Five, Pat's Relationship Realm, where she set goals, prepared her to create a project to assist her in getting involved in activities where she would have the opportunity to meet men who fit her description. Remember, she is fully committed to the possibility that this astounding relationship can be a reality. (She is grounded in it.)

Her project involves creating a group of like-minded people to begin a community endeavor to contribute to underprivileged kids who never get to experience nature and wilderness adventures. In Session One we used Pat's values as examples: she valued Adventure, Beauty and

Love. Since adventure is paramount to her, something she intensely desires in her life experience, there is a good chance she will meet a man who shares her love of the outdoors and the challenges associated with outdoor adventure as a result of her project. She has a dual purpose. She is passionate about making a difference for young kids and she desires a wonderful love relationship. So, combining those purposes in a project that could very well provide the worthy companion she seeks as well as establish a source of abundant adventure for young people certainly contributes to her Realm. Her project enables her to *be* her natural abilities.

To begin, she assesses the activities she will need to generate to make this project real. She will need volunteers and interested participants. She will need an outing or adventure experience for the kids to attend. Who will be the attendees? Where will she locate the kids? How will she get people involved?

Since she is a real estate agent and is already actively involved in a Boys' and Girls' Club in her community, she has a great opportunity to begin speaking about her project.

Her passionate enthusiasm will attract the appropriate people to assist her cause.

She has decided to begin by creating a brochure describing her project and summoning interested people to come on board. She is going to sponsor a wine and cheese evening in her home for a presentation of her project. She uses her real estate network and her Boys' and Girls' Club affiliation as the starting point of recruiting possible committee members. Once she creates and distributes her brochure, she intends to speak to several community organizations regarding the project and the specific requests for contributions to get it launched.

She has put together some pages in her organizer that describe her project. This method helps her to chart her progress and stay focused on each idea and intention.

PAT'S SAMPLE PROJECT PAGES

Her first page is labeled with the name she has given her project. She also identifies the Realm her project supports.

Unlock Your Heart: Goal Setting from the Inside Out

Date: March 10, 2000
Project: Outdoor Youth Adventures
Realm: Rich Intimate Relationships
Purpose: To bring adventure and excitement to underprivileged kids and create an opportunity to experience love and adventure with a wonderful man.

<u>My commitment to the project</u>:

I am committed to being the energy it takes to enroll others in a wilderness adventure program for kids. I am committed to creating an astounding relationship with a wonderful man who shares my love of adventure and my desire to serve others.

<u>My goals as intentions</u>:

1) I intend to establish a committee to generate time, energy and resources to launch this project.
2) I intend to find the perfect place to have the wilderness experience.

Jane Ellen Davis

3) I intend to meet an interesting man who shares my love and passion for adventure and for contributing to kids.
4) I intend for this project to be endorsed by several large fundraising organizations.
5) I intend for people to get excited and assist me in any way they can.

She describes the project as if it was already actively happening and she includes a powerful end result. As she begins activating the project goals she will structure her actions from her desired end result.

Outdoor Youth Adventures has taken several outstanding trips to The Grand Canyon River Rafting, Yosemite, An Outward Bound weekend, and soon will be going to New Mexico. There are five sponsors already in place and over $200,000 has been raised. 750 children have already benefited from the outdoor adventures. A very powerful, wonderful man has taken over the chairman position and he and I are spending quality time together in a loving relationship.

She establishes a completion date: January 10, 2002. From there she begins describing the action steps she and others must take to create the energy and the resources necessary to generate the project.

ACTION STEPS

1) I am designing a brochure to distribute to advertise my project.
2) I am giving presentations to clubs and organizations.
3) A volunteer has created a web site for the project and interested people are responding.
4) I am making at least 5-10 phone calls daily to enroll interested volunteers.
5) I am specifically requesting men who are dedicated to making a difference for young people who would never experience adventure in the outdoors; preferably single men who could devote the time, energy and resources for the project.

Notice her action steps are stated clearly as a commitment. Remember, she is passionately enrolled in the idea that the project is a reality and that the desired result has been achieved. So these actions become exciting and joyous. They are not viewed as laborious tasks.

Pat also decided to create an Items To Be List. She was quite accustomed to using an Items To Do list, but she felt that the To Be List would keep her more focused on her values.

TO BE LIST

1. Be a loving listener
2. Be enthusiastic
3. Be aware of the beauty around me
4. Be patient with myself and others

Now that Pat's action steps are defined and declared, she is ready to generate energy, resources and time. This is where the practical doing takes place.

While keeping her focus on her core values, she will access each action step and decide how much of her energy will be required to generate momentum. She will think through the necessary resources she needs. She will schedule time to devote to these action steps.

For example, one of her action steps states: "I am designing a brochure to distribute to advertise my project." She must assess how much of her creative energy will be required to design her brochure. She must decide who she will need to assist her. She needs to clarify approximately how much money will be needed to fund the brochure.

Once she has completed her assessment, she will go to her weekly calendar and block out time to do the action steps. The beauty of a project method of planning is the clarity it brings. There is nothing vague about Pat's plan. She knows exactly what her purpose is and it is clearly connected to her values. She <u>really</u> wants this project to be a reality. Her vision fuels her determination and her enthusiasm will be embraced by others with similar goals and values.

Pat may choose to create several projects to support her Relationship Realm. She will plan her projects according to the amount of time she can devote to pursuing each one. If each Realm has several projects designed to support that Realm, time management will definitely be a factor. She

Jane Ellen Davis

will probably decide to focus on her most passionate Realms first.

Unlock Your Heart: Goal Setting from the Inside Out

MASTER PLAN PROJECT PAGE

Date: _____

Project: _____
_____

Realm: _____
_____

Purpose: _____
_____
_____
_____
_____
_____
_____

My commitment to my project: _____
_____
_____
_____
_____

Jane Ellen Davis

My goals stated as intentions: _____

_____

_____

_____

_____

_____

_____

_____

_____

_____

Describe the project as if it was already actively happening including the end result:

_____

_____

_____

_____

_____

_____

_____

_____

Unlock Your Heart: Goal Setting from the Inside Out

Establish a completion date: _____

_____

Describe the action steps necessary to generate the project:

ACTION STEPS

_____

_____

_____

_____

_____

_____

ITEMS TO BE LIST

1. _____

_____

2. _____

_____

Jane Ellen Davis

3. _____

   _____

4. _____

   _____

Follow this format for each project you create based on your Realms. As you become more enrolled in your projects and begin to see your Realms materializing, your enthusiasm for this method of planning will increase. Session Seven will assist you in recognizing your outstanding improvements. Owning your values and living them is a very fulfilling process.

Unlock Your Heart: Goal Setting from the Inside Out

Session Seven

Charting Your Progress

This is the reward you have been working toward. Here you will acknowledge yourself for whom you have chosen to become. You will create a way to chart your progress. You will complete, in the moment, that which you have been manifesting. Life for you now is exciting, invigorating, full, rich and fun. It is that way because you have been willing to move through old limiting beliefs, behaviors that have kept you stuck, relationships that were belittling or made you feel less than; and whatever else was in your way. You realized very early in session one and two that you had a choice. The work was not about changing someone, it was about shifting from an old attitude or belief, and embracing a new, empowering belief that contributed unlimited possibilities to who you are. You did it—you chose the freedom to be creative and live a rich, passionate life. It is time to acknowledge yourself for being willing to embrace this process and grow.

Jane Ellen Davis

Remember the Wheel of Purpose you did in Session One? Here it is again. Do the same process and see the wonderful progress you have made. No doubt you will have more eights and nines now, maybe even some tens! Once you have completed the wheel and have compared it with your first wheel, you will want to acknowledge yourself. The wheel exercise provides you with visual proof of your progress.

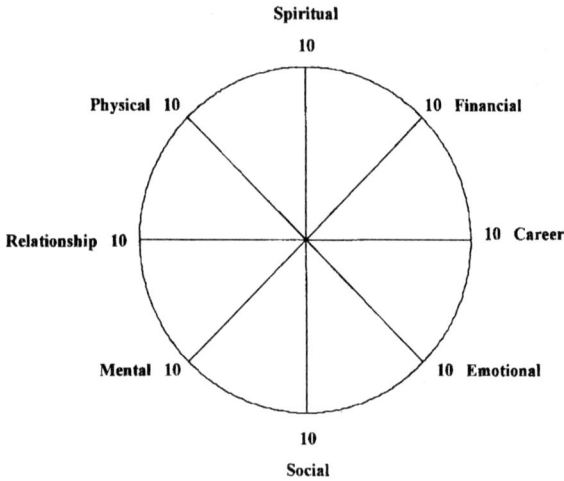

Place a dot on the line that best indicates where you are right now in each realm of your life. 0 being the lowest--10 being the highest. Then connect the dots. What do you see about your balance and purpose? What will it take to create a 10 in each area? Who will you need to *be*?

Unlock Your Heart: Goal Setting from the Inside Out

CHARTING YOUR PROGRESS

Let us create a way for you to chart your progress. For each person, this will be different. My way of charting may not work as well as one you design for yourself. Here is your chance to design a system that works for you. I will simply supply guidelines.

You will be working closely with your master plan from Session Six. Since you will be using that plan to keep you focused on your various projects, your charting will be based on that plan.

It is important that you acknowledge yourself for completing actions that serve your intentions. Each time an aspect of your desired purpose becomes a reality you will want to note the completion on your chart. The main goal of Session Seven is for you to be able to see how empowered you have become. It will give you a visual way to pat yourself on the back and continue to be empowered and successful in your purposes. It will also serve as a way to catch yourself if you get off track with your desires and projects. I am including a few sample methods other clients have developed as a way to chart their progress.

Jane Ellen Davis

Pat decided the most important part of her projects to monitor was the intentions she had created. She devised a page in her organizer specifically for recording the completion of her intentions.

EXAMPLE

INTENTIONS COMPLETED FOR PROJECT:
Outdoor Youth Adventures

- ☑ I found the perfect place for the wilderness experience.
- ☑ Several fund raising groups have endorsed my project.

She found that this form of acknowledgment helped her to stay motivated. With each completion she was able to see her progress.

She also wanted to keep track of her action steps. She used a highlighting marker to indicate the completion of each action step. They are listed in her organizer, so she simply lined out each one as she completed it. This saved her time—she wasn't double writing.

Unlock Your Heart: Goal Setting from the Inside Out

Kristy, a client who loves creative visual tools, developed a Success Journal. Her journal is a book with blank pages. She keeps it by her bed and every night before retiring, she writes down her successes. She has a collection of motivational stickers to enhance the pages. Her journal allows her to acknowledge her achievements. The action of writing each night keeps her focused on her purpose. She enjoys the practice and loves being creative with the stickers. The important point is that this technique works for Kristy.

Suzanne likes to use gold stars and places them next to completed goals and intentions. She keeps a large chart over her desk. Each Realm and Project is listed. When she achieves her intentions within a project, she puts a gold star on the chart. This method gives her a visual appreciation of her actions. This technique also keeps her focused on her priorities within each Realm.

Those of you who are more analytical and linear may need to design a graph to chart your progress. If you are accustomed to using your computer, you will probably want to create a graph on one of your programs.

Jane Ellen Davis

Dan, a client who is very analytical and logical, created a graph to acknowledge himself. One of his most passionate Realms is Abundant Harvest. He and his wife, Dee, have a dream of creating a farm that supplies food for the needy. Recently they have moved to a five-acre plot and have begun to manifest their dream. They are operating on a limited budget and understand that this will be a long-term project.

Dan liked the idea of a chart set up to illustrate his goals and intentions. Since several steps are required to reach completion of each goal, he puts an X next to each complete step.

This visual exercise keeps him on target with his intentions. He finds that due to his clarity of purpose and focus, he is able to speak to others about his project. As a result of his enthusiasm and clarity, several other people have expressed an interest in assisting him. Dan and Dee discovered that their passion for making this food project a reality has enrolled others in participating.

Unlock Your Heart: Goal Setting from the Inside Out

DAN'S ABUNDANT HARVEST PROJECT

X	Step 1	Contact interested individuals for planning meeting.
X	Step 2	Have a planning meeting – types of crops to be planted, etc.
	Step 3	Establish fund for planting materials.
	Step 4	Set up committees for planting, fertilizing, weeding and harvesting.
	Step 1	Prepare acre plot for planting.
	Step 2	Plant crops.
	Step 3	
	Step 4	
	Step 1	Fertilize crops.
	Step 2	Weed crops.
	Step 3	
	Step 4	

Darlene has devised a photo board to accompany her Natural Teacher Realm. Since her intention is to create travel experiences for groups, she decided to use her photo talents to inspire her planning. She designed a poster board with photos she has taken that represent the places she will take people. She collects brochures, pamphlets, etc., that show the tours and sights they will visit. As she enrolls people in a trip, she puts their names on the board. She can also use the board when she gives lectures to promote her trips. One interesting benefit of this method is that she rediscovered her love of photography. She intends to have her trips include an emphasis on photojournalism.

A NEW WAY OF BEING

As you begin to create your own way of tracking your progress you want to be able to check in with yourself daily. You must acknowledge what you accomplish each day within all your Realms. The key is to get excited about the difference you made in your area of passion and purpose. Many times it will appear small or simple, but if you are truly standing for that greatness it will happen. Others will contribute their energy. It will not all be up to you. Your contribution may be as simple as an encouraging word, a prayer, a vision of the greatest possibility, perhaps speaking your vision to someone—the point is, notice and acknowledge when you have stood fast in *being* your vision. You have remained grounded in that vision.

Now that you have completed the sessions, your life is no doubt fuller, richer, and more empowered. As you continue to develop your Realms and your projects grow, you will embrace this process quite naturally. Your Realms will change as you progress.

Unlock Your Heart: Goal Setting from the Inside Out

You are well on your way to making a difference in the quality of your own life and the lives of those around you. You have truly unlocked your heart. Enjoy Yourself! You have a delightful journey ahead!

Printed in the United States
1815